THE ONE WHO FAILED

SHADOWS OF FEAR

SHEKHAR BODA

A negative story which hits in a positive way. It dives deep into what happens in life if you can't over come from fear.

Contents

FOREWORD

Preface

This is the story about the young boy who struggles with fear. His fears hold him back and he finds it hard to overcome them.He's scared of many things , As we follow his journey we see how his fear affects his relationships with his friends and family, his school life, and his daily struggles. Its about a boy who faces his fear every day and how he tries to live with them.This story is not about winning or achieving success. It's all about how fear effects in our lifes and what happens if we can't overcome from it. A negative story which hits in a positive way

Acknowledgements

To you the reader from the deepest part of my heart thank you thank you for picking up this book for choosing to spend your precious time whitin these pages Thank you for being a part of this journey your presence as a reader are the ultimate reward

About The Author

SHEKHAR NAYAK

Meet Shekhar, Literature and Fiction Writer born on August 25th, 2001, His journey as a writer began with his debut ebook, "Martin, The Prince of Kepler," which marked the starting point of his passion project to create moral stories for children and adults alike.With a keen interest in crafting fiction stories that not only entertain but also convey valuable life lesson

"On instagram as @iamshekharnayak"

Stay tuned for more exciting stories from Shekhar, as he continues to weave his magic with words! Follow Shekhar's writing journey

I

THE FIRST CRY

John was a businessman he wanted to be rich and live a great life, He always wanted make more money he never said no to money John worked hard every day, He made smart decisions to make more money. John's goal was to be wealthy and he wanted to be famous and live a luxurious life.

John's life was about money he loved the feeling of success he would do whatever it took to be rich and always work for it. But John believed in something more than just hard work he believed in luck he thought luck plays a big role in his success but ? his friends and family members are always worried about him and suggest him to be careful but John never listen to them he always focused on his success John's life is all about money.

"He used to trade in stock market every time and also do different kind of business to earn more money".

John's parents wanted him to get married they chose a girl named Martha where, John's parents want to get control his money mind at least he may get married so they decided John to get married to Martha.

John met Martha, she was kind and nice women. John liked her he agreed to marry her.

One fine day, John and Martha got married. John's parents were happy after John marring to Martha. But Martha couldn't change

John's mind about money.

Days passed, suddenly John's business started to fail. His shares went down he lost a lot of money John was very worried he did not know what to do. He tried to fix his business but did not worked he was loosing everything and he did not know how to get back where, he lost more and more money. He couldn't pay his bills so, the bank took his house and all his propertys. John shifted to a small house he had gone rich man to a poor man he did not know how to get back on his feet.

Months passed, Martha got pregnant and John was happy but also worried, He did not have much money to take care of her so, John decided to leave Martha to her parents house so they can take care of her. Finally the day arrived Martha was admitted to hospital.

Martha's parents informs to John, That Martha got admitted to hospital. John rushed to hospital and worried about Martha and the baby and waited nervously outside of operation room. The doctor came out with a big smile "Congratulations" The doctor said, you blessed with a baby boy. John felt very happy and rushed into the operation room to see Martha and the baby boy John was felling very happy after looking at Martha and the boy.

The boy was crying very loudly John and Martha feeling very happy. At the same time John got a call that he got a big business deal he felt very happy! and his shares went up very high at the same time.

His business started growing all his lost property came back to him John was very happy and get back to his lost house he thought about the baby boy he believed that the baby boy brought him luck and thought very lucky to have him so, he decided to named as Victor . Victor meaning victory and success John life was changed again he was very happy about his baby boy Victor who brings his luck back to him

John and Martha were very happy about Victor and John though Victor will bring more money and success John believed his luck would continue to grow so, John kept high exceptions on Victor

He thought Victor would make him more richer.

John Belived in luck he tought victor brought luck to him

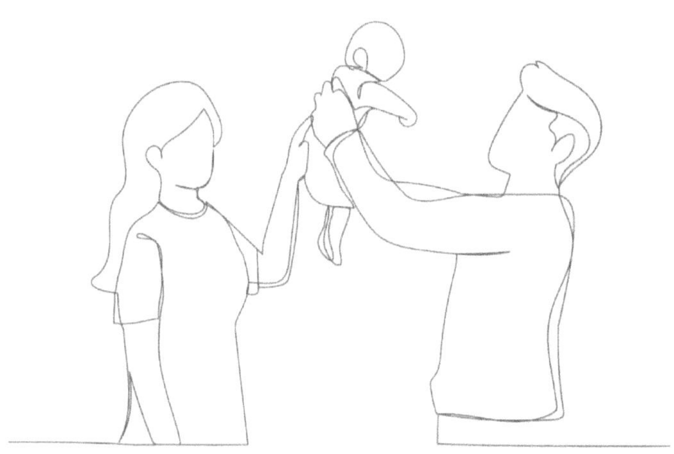

"Believe time changes everything"

II

THE BOY VICTOR

As days are passing, John became very successful in his business and became very rich and victor grow up now he was 8 years old, his play schooling has completed shifting to an primary school. John always wanted to give best to victor .

But victor was very quit kid he did not talk much and he also scared to go to school and also afraid to share his thoughts and feelings he did not like to trouble others and not an active kid like other kids

John and Martha worried about Victor's silence they wanted him to open up to share his thoughts and feelings but victor was afraid so he kept quit and his silence made him lonely and always remain as silent and he was too shy to talk so, he doesn't talk to much. John decided to join victor in best school and

change his mindset John decided to join victor in best school

John took victor to school on his first day but victor was nervous he did not want to go to school he hold Johns hand tightly ,feeling scared John tried to calm him down and victor was. worried they walked to the class room victor looked around seeing new faces feeling nervous

John : its ok son don't feel nervous

They reached near to the class room door victor was nervous he looked up to his father John where, victor's eyes are with tears John said don't worry

I will be hear, I will wait out side you get into the classroom ok.

Victor took a deep breath and slowly walked into classroom, He looked around seeing kids chatting laughing and playing in class.

Victor felt very shy and don't know what to say he saw the teacher and the teacher said hello! kid come, and sit. Victor was a little bit worried and looked back to his father but his father was not there at the door step victor was worried and started crying and but, the teacher came forward and hold the victor's hand and led him back to his seat. The teacher gently asked to victor what happen ,don't cry see every one is looking at you so sit quietly victor sat quietly in his place the teacher asked victor what is your name kid

Victor did not answered he was worried he never spoke to an unknown person, victor remains silent this time the teacher shouted toward victor hello kid i asking too you what's your name?

Victor answered : yes, mam victor answered with low voice

Teacher : ok victor don't cry your dad will come by the evening

Victor was not listening to his teacher he was thinking about, why ? his father lied to him he said that, I will stat outside where, victor's dad

John wanted to make him strong and smart he know's that it was not that much easy but victor worried and thinking about it and time passed quickly and the day ended.

John came to pickup victor smiling and feeling happy but victor was not happy at all he just get inside the car and sat silently when they went home John asked victor how was your first day he did not answer Martha also asked but victor did not answer to them John ok it his first day to leave us so he may be worried.

John and Martha sat for dinner with victor but, same victor did not answer and looked down

> *"John : ok victor it's time for bed you have to go school tomorrow*
>
> *John made a promise himself to be more supportive to victor.*
>
> *But victor was always worried himself."*

Days turned into weeks and weeks turned into months but, victor was still struggled with fear and low confidence. He didn't belive in himself Victor's lack of low confidence held him back in every way he was afried to try new things and always a self doubt boy. Victor's studies were poor he struggled to understand

" Luck is great but most of Life is Hard work"

III
HIGH SCHOOL

Victor grew up, now he was VI class and shifted from primary school to high school but the grades didn't improve he got average marks and every teacher scolded him John was very disappointed he wanted victor to be smarter and brighter student.

"But victor was not interested in studies."

One day were. Victor did not completed his daily homework he was worrying at the night and thinking how to skip the school tomorrow and he got a plan to skip the school and went to sleep. The sun rises Martha knock the door of victor's room to wakeup him and get ready for school but victor did not wake up So, Martha came and asked Victor what happened

"Victor : I'm not feeling well mom i think I'm suffering from fever"

"Martha said to John victor was suffering from fever lets call the doctor"

Dr.Mick who was John's family doctor came to there home.

Dr.Mick said, Victor you don't have fever you are fine but victor said but i'm not feeling well, and I'm suffring from stomachache then Dr.Mick for stomachache I will give few tablets and take rest everything will be ok. John and Martha are discussing what happened to him suddenly he was fine and looking good where, last night but victor was thinking about school that his parents will decide let him stay at home and take rest or they will say go to school.

John said, Victor take rest for two days you will get recover victor from inside he was feeling very happy he can now skip the school. Day passes victor went to school on the following day asked his friend what teacher said did everyone completed the work victor's bad luck his friend said that the teacher did not came to school yesterday. Victor shocked and started worrying the class bell rang its the teacher first hour who gave home work and all students went to class and the class started victor was worrying and thinking about the homework the teacher started the class suddenly the class representative reminded about the homework to teacher

> *"The teacher : ok students who did't completed the work please standup"*

Victor looks down and feeling guilty.

Teacher : okay students, I will check one by one now so standup Victor and other two students where stood up

Teacher : okay you three did not completed your work so, get out of the classroom and stand outside.

Victor and other two students stranded outside of the classroom

Victor feeling guilty that he was thinking why I did not completed the work this should be the last time, from tomorrow onwards I should complete the work on time suddenly, the school principal came to rounds and saw the students standing outside of the classroom.

> *"Principal : asked the teacher , what's going on here why are these students standing outside"*

> *"Teacher : Good Morning sir, these students did not completed there work so I made them to stand out side of class"*

Principal : I see well but this is not the right thing giving punishment is not correcting them give them an additional work or any other think which up skill them

Okay, tell them to report to the assembly tomorrow and lead the school song and pledge

Ok students don't repeat it again

The teacher given pledge to victor and school prayer to other students victor started thinking in his mind pledge how can I say and that to in front of all students.

"Teacher : ok students come to school early tomorrow you should conduct school assembly ."

" Fear leads to Failure "

"

ॐ

IV
THE STAGE FRIGHT

Victor was given the pledge to say in front of the whole school, He was very feared he did not want to do it he practiced at home but he was not confident at all he also tried to skip the school but his father said no to him.

Victor went to school and the assembly started, the school prayer was said now its victor's turn.

His plans were sweating too he did not want to tell the pledge but he know he had to face he took a deep breath and started to say the pledge but his voice was shaking a bit he fumbled and said a wrong word the entire school started laughing.

Victor felt embarrassed he felt like he had failed he stopped back and walked away

The principle called victor to his office after the assemble, he motivated victor don't worry just be calm he called victor parents and told what happened

John was very upset and angry John said, "victor you can't even say a simple pledge how will you achieve in life.

Martha tried to calm down John Don't worry but John was worried he wanted victor to overcome his fear Victor felt sad, he did not know how to overcome his stage fear. The principle said victor you need to practice and face fear you should practice stood in front of the mirror and spoke to yourself first practice, practice

John took Victor home feeling disappointed and sad, victor needs extra classes would help to getup in his life he needs to learn to be brave and he decided to join victor in extra evening classes.

John said victor you are going to extra classes from tomorrow Victor worried and thinking about the extra classes and feeling sad.

John said,

" Victor life is full of ups and downs but you cant let your fears hold you back you need to face your fears you need to be brave and strong always remember it's ok to make mistake that's how we learn

and grow victor listening to his dad but he is still thinking about what happened at the assembly

John said never give up victor I'm always with you I'm hear to support you and guide you Victor hugged John feeling grateful for his fathers love and support.

The next day victor went to school feeling nervous and scared. The students started laughing at him victor felt bad and guilty the students teased him hey victor you messed up the pledge victor looked down and feeling sad.

The teacher tried to stop! the students but, the students wouldn't listen. Victor felt like crying he just wanted to go home. He just wanted to be alone

But suddenly remembered what his father said then he took a deep breath and stood up straight he looked at the student and said I'm sorry I messed Up but I will try again the students stopped laughing they looked at victor surprise the teacher smiled and said Thats the sprit Victor.

Victor felt a little better he felt he had taken a step forward he realised he had to be strong he had to be brave He walked back to his seat feeling a little more confident he know he still had a lot to learn the principle came to class and called victor.

How are you feeling now ? are you ok ?victor said

Yes sir, I'm ok

Principle said Are you ready to try again

"Victor : Yes sir"

This time victor felt more confident he practiced a lot, he stood in front of mirror he practiced

The next day, Victor stood on

stage he took a deep breath and remembered, what his father said and started

He finished the pledge without a mistake Victor smiled and feeling happy.

After completing school assembly the principal called victor and said,

"*Principal : victor i want you to know that everyone learns differently no two people have same ability to learn*

"when i was child, i had to read and write ten times to remember them but the point is everyone can learn and remember for me it took ten times for few it may took one time it's different we just need to find our abilitie and what works best to us"."

" *Practice does not make perfect perfect practice makes you perfect* "

V

THE THREE FRIENDS

Days passes, victor continued to go to school daily he made new friends

Max and Steve were they became his bench mate too.

Max was a very good boy, He always do his work on time, He is very responsible and helped victor with his homework. Steve on the other hand he was a little bit lazy he often didn't work and copy from Max and Victor liking hanging out with both of them.

They would play together and having lunch together the three friends continued to hang out together they support and help each other Victor was very happy to have Max and Steve as friends and go to each other's house for playing and also used to play online games daily from home exams were coming and they decided to study hard max said lets stop playing for few days after exams, we can start again but Steve would call victor and max to play online games but max was not interested max want to study hard and want to get good marks but Steve and victor started playing even on the night before the exam max warn them but they did not listened they played games until late night before the exam day On the exam day three of them went to School and the exam started.

Max was very confident about the exam but, victor was a little bit worried because he did not studied at all the exam started max was writing the exam confidently but, victor was nervous he did not know any of the answers at all he looked at Steve he was also writing the exam confidently but victor didn't understand how he was writing with out studying for exam Victor still did not started the exam he does not know what to write there is still ten minutes remaining for completing the exam time victor thinking what to write feeling very nervous.

He just filled the same questions in the answer paper which was given the question paper, the time is up victor handed the answer sheet to the teacher, after completing the exam victor asked the Steve hay, Steve you did not studied for the exam how did you write Victor smiled and answered I copied the exam well victor had not done well but he did not know how badly he had failed the next day teacher announced the exam results max got the top marks in the class and Steve also got good marks teacher looked at victors paper.

and called him and asked you didn't written anything on the paper and you simple copied same questions from the questions paper the teacher decided to give punishment to victor and called the victor's parents and complained about his behaviour and said what he wrote on the exam paper John and Martha were disappointed and feeling sad about victor.

Victor why did you do that ? John asked

Principle advised he need to learn how to study and take exam seriously make sure he should understand how important education is but, he does not listened to them and the principled warned if you do not improve you should repeat the year and study the same class again victor felt ashamed and sorry for his behaviour he promised him self that he should do better next time. John got a call from his office about his business deals he hurried and went to office.

" Good or bad it always depends on you "

VI
THE BAD LUCK

On the same day, John's business started to fail and he lost all his money he had to sell his big house and move to small house again

John was worried and sad he felt like he has lost everything Martha tried to help him bit he was demotivated and John worried about victor school fees that there is no income and how he should pay the fees of victor' school.

Martha decided to work as a primary school teacher, to support the family John was proud but he still a failure John and Martha didn't change victor's school they wanted him to have a good education and a better future John still believed in victor days passed now victor was in high school Martha was helping victor daily in his home work and supporting him victor felt very bad about his father business loss and he decided to study hard victor final exams arrived and he studied hard he wanted to make his parents proud and pass with good marks max on other hand was confident of topping the class he also study hard throughout the year and well prepared.

Steve however was worried He had relied on copying throughout the year but the final exams were strict and he knew he couldn't copy the day of the result arrived and victor was nervous he had done his best but he wasn't sure if it was enough and finally the exam's started victor and max prepare for final exams and Steve did not prepare for exams this time victor and max confidently written all the exams and did well but Steve had no chance to copy the exams.

The day of results arrived and victor was nervous he had done his best but he was not sure that if it was enough results announced three of them gathered together and checking there result.

First max entered his hall ticket numbered for result he got highest marks and he felt.

Very happy! about it and next, max entered Steve number were Steve also know he did not done well in exams the result opened he failed.

Victor and Max were feeling very sad about Steve and now it's victor turn max entered victor's number the result page is started buffering victor was feeling nervous that Steve has failed is there any chance if I also failed my parents won't feel happy the result was opened he was passed with an average marks but he was feeling happy about it and informed to there parents Martha felt very happy about it but John was not at all happy because he got an average marks!.

John finally said okay! It's ok victor the high school has completed now, the real journey begins you have to join in a good college and start focus on your life and settled with a good job Martha replayed to John what John job you didn't involving him in business why

John sadly said no because I faced a lot of struggle and failed what have nothing remains we lost everything in my life ok and John congratulate to max for getting good marks and said I'm felling very happy about you max I wish I could had a son like you but victor was not happy about what John said to max

he started hating max John advised both of them to John in same college max said ok uncle we will and I will always with victor.

John also feeling sad about Steve and also give advised don't worry life is not only about studies there is lot of many things why don't you start again and repeat the same year of class but Steve did not listen to him he silently left from there.

But victor was confused about his dad he did not tell anything to Steve ok let it be,

Victor and Max decided to join same college.

• 24 •

" *Believe in Hard work* "

❧

VII
COLLEGE LIFE

Victor promise his father, I will do well and get the best job and mom can retire

Max got admission in best college but, victor did not get admission in the same college due to his less marks John used his old influence he got the admission too.

On the first day of college, Victor and Max went to college and entered into class but victor did not sat along with max

First day first call max felt happy and victor was trying to make new friends and he used to start avoiding max.

The next day, of college Victor got new friend name Ben.

Victor studied hard in his first year of college and did well in his exams, He has good ability to study but he did not overcome from the fear ant still lack of low confidence and still he step backward when ever it comes to any class presentations or stage performances, He still has the stage fear but never tries to over come from it he has doubt in every aspect. He used to think twice to do any think he checks every time but he got good marks and happy with his performance but as the days passed and victor started enjoying with he used to skip the classes and go out with his friends and got addicted to new habits max tried to convey victor to not do such things but victor does not listen to him.

But, "when the exams came around Victor was not prepared he had not attend classes and had not studied and he failed his exams".

John was disappointed and sad he had hopping that victor would make a better life he thought he is the lucky one he has but John said its ok you can try again it not over of your college.

But victor does not listen to him he continued to skip the classes, He did not change his ways he started enjoying his life with his friends Ben and victor became very close. Ben also a fun loving person and encourage victor to skip the classes together.

But deep down victor know he was making mistake he was trowing away his future and max always warn victor to don't to do such things on day max decided to tell to victor's parents about his behaviour in college and went to victor's house he said everything to John where he is not coming to classes and he has changed his habits and not at all studying and coming to classes at all John was heartbroken after listen to Max what he says he lost all the hope he had on victor.

John felt like he was reliving his own failures he don't know how to help victor he felt like he was loosing his son Martha tried to stay positive she still believe in victor but John lost the hope in victor and started avoiding victor and stops caring about him and started avoiding to talk but victor does not care about any think at all.

" One real friend is better than thousand fake friends "

VIII
THE SPORTS CLUB

One day, The sports association in college had announced an event victor was not interested but Ben was very excited as he was very good at sports Ben asked Victor

> "*Ben : Hey victor have you every played football*
> *Victor : No*
> *Ben : why don't we go for selections in football team for college*
> *Victor : sorry i was not interested In playing any game or sport*"

You can go for selection

Ben decided to go and he got selected in collage team

That he was trained well in football from his childhood and also played in his school days

Ben selected on the football team finally the event was started and the guests has arrived

Ben played a fantastic

game and score highest goals from his team a lead to win the game and helped to win college team to win the league Ben was the highest goal scorer from the tournament

One of the guest was a selector for national football team. He impressed with Ben's game and selected him for national football A team

He called, Ben and said that I'm selecting you for football Jr. team A for national level Ben was very exited he was feeling very surprised

"*Victor asked to Ben*"

"*Victor : why are you so happy it's just a game*

Ben : this is a big opportunity for me I can also get a chance in national team if play a good game

Ben success had made victor realise that he need to find his passion"

He realised that he need to find his own passion in life he started thinking

What I'm good at.

He realised that he did not played anything he did not played any sport or learned any music instrument.

" Talent is a gift but character is a choice "

IX

THE BAD PHASE OF LIFE

One more year left to complete his collage life were, He tried to study hard again and got passed with an average marks the campus selections has started he also got a chance for an interview.

"Finally victor went to interview"

"Interviewer : Good morning
Victor : Good Morning sir
Interviewer : tell me about yourself"

Victor nervously said his name but, cant even get a conversation and don't know what to say

That was a disappointment interview he was not confident at all he left the interview room he got dis qualified.

Days passed, victor completed his collage life He graduated with average marks and he did not get selected and did not get any Job.

But his friend, Max was selected and got a high paying Job Victor was very dissatisfied about him Ben also got selected in national team but victor left nothing to do he would just sit at home idle and useless John was very disappointed about him Martha was still continuing her Job.

John with his influence tried to get a job for victor He called up his old friend Mr Tomas who was working as a manager in a big company Thomas agreed to give a job to victor and he has hired without any interview victor got into training period

Victor did not take the job seriously he did not learn anything during his training period Thomas was disappointed with victor's performance, He did not expected this from John's son

Thomas called Victor,

Thomas : Victor you are taking this Job seriously

Victor : "I'm sorry, sir I will try to do better

Victor tried many time to learn but due to lack of his low confidence he can't any thing and he was unable to remember anything

After getting into his job,

Thomas was not satisfied with his performance and he got fired, John was disappointed and sad after he herd the news.

Victor did not understand why he gotten removed from his job and he did not know what to do next.

Martha called Victor and said

"Martha : hey victor do you remember when you wear learning to ride a cycle as a kid

Victor : yes mom i remember

Martha : you fell down so many times times but you never gaveup why

Victor : i don't know i just wanted to learn

Martha : exactly you had passion to learn and you belived in yourself you know you could ride that cycle

well life is just like learning to ridee you are going to falldown sometimes but you can't gave up and belive in yourself.
"

" Self Confidence is a super power "

X
THE OLD FRIEND

"One day, victor went to a restaurant there he saw his old friend Steve sitting at a table

    Victor : Steve long time good to see you

    How are you ?

    Steve : I'm good, and what about you ?

    Victor : I have been ok, I guess

    I just graduate from college but I haven't been abel to find a job yet

    Steve : sorry, to hear that

    But, I have a solution for you I am thinking of starting a business and I am looking for a partner

    Victor : really, what kind of business ?

    Steve : I am thinking to buy ,this restaurant thats why I came to this place

    Victor: That's sounds like a great idea

    But what I need to do

    Steve : you need to investment on it to get partnership"

Victor said ok to Steve

Victor went to his dad and asked for money to invest in Steve business

But John was not impressed with the idea he said you don't even know victor if Steve's business would succeed John was refused to gave money

Martha felt sad and decided to help his son business idea she decided to give money to victor and took a loan from bank and gave to victor

Victor immediately gave money to Steve and get back to home the next day he went to the restaurant for Steve he was not there and he made call where Steve was not answering his calls and he asked to restaurant manager about him about Steve that said we don't know who he is we are sorry

He said he made a deal to buy this restaurant and I gave him money to and the restaurant manager said this place was not for sell and we are not had a deal to any one. Victor was shock he don't know what to say

Victor was heartbroken and don't know what to do he don't know Steve was a fraud he went to his parents and told them what happened John was disappointed and angry over Martha why you gave money to victor

Victor don't know what to do John gave a complaint in police station and later the police find Steve and refunded the money to Victor .

" Don't trust anyone blindly "

"From there victor did not get any job and started living in his house . Victor's life has taken a disappointing he had failed to achieve any think his friend max studied hard and got a good job and he settled well and Ben also became notional player in football team but Victor was struggled with low confidence which held him back to achieve his carrier and he has also failed to deliver on his promise and had not made any progress in life his father John was very disappointed about him lack of low confidence of victor had lead him to failure he felt lost and aloneAs he realised on his life that he need to make a change over his fear he needed to start believing him self and his abilitiesHe wish he would had a chance that he can make changes from his childhood that want to believe in himself and confident and also want to participate in sports and games and study good and work hard but as of now he can not change any thing which already happen he just need to find a new way.

The One Who Failed"

Written by

SHEKHAR NAYAK

Shadows Of Fear And Failure

He wish, he would had a chance to change everythink but he cant change the past

if you would have a chance to change then change now loose fear and be confident

because fear leads to failure

BHASI BA - THE PRICE OF DARKNESS

Bhasi Ba - The Price Of Darkness

A poor woodcutter, becomes rich. But as he gets more money, he starts to change. Will he stay a kind and good person, or will the money make him mean and selfish? This book tells the story of how money can change someone, for better or worse.

Written by

"—— *Shekhar Nayak*"

Preface Of Bhasi Ba

Joseph is a woodcutter living in a small, peaceful village with a small family were his wife, Leena and their two children, Rohan and Rina. Every day, Joseph heads into the nearby forest, where he cuts wood to sell in the local market. His life is very simple and routine of his work

Bhasi Ba The Price Of Darkness

Joseph the Woodcutter

Joseph is a woodcutter living in a small, peaceful village with a small family were his wife, Leena and their two children, Rohan and Rina. Every day, Joseph heads into the nearby forest, where he cuts wood to sell in the local market. His life is very simple and routine of his work

Joseph finds happiness in the little things Joseph was a humble man who always wanted to earn money to support his family and himself. He had big dreams for a better life, and he was determined to work hard to achieve them. Every day, he would wake up early, before the sun rise, to head into the forest and cut wood. He was a hard working person With every piece of wood he cut, Joseph felt like he was one step closer to achieving his dreams.

One day, Joseph went far into the forest, deeper than usual, and he found a tree that looked very valuable. and he started cutting the tree with his axe, while cutting down the axe head suddenly slipped and fell on his hand, Joseph was injured and started bleed.were His blood drops fall upon the tree, were the tree started to absorb the blood and slowly began to glow. Joseph stepped backward and looking at the tree and suddenly a piece of gold was fallen from the tree Joseph surprise, and took the piece of gold Suddenly, the tree makes some terrifying noise, Joseph Shocked and holding his breath with lots of fear ,and shouted loudly towards the tree "Who are you? Are you really a tree?" Are you making the noise, suddenly The tree replied,

Yes I'm BHASI BA

BHASI BA THE KING

I am BHASI BA once I was a king, but I was cursed by God for being greedy and cruel. I wanted to be the richest king ever and wanted all the gold and I didn't care about my people. They suffered and died due to lack of food and water because I didn't help them. Now, I'm a tree. I have the power to give gold, but only if I get human blood. The more blood, the more gold. But I'm trapped - I can't use the gold, I can only give it. I'm punished for my past mistakes. I was selfish and hurt my people, now I'm a tree, giving gold, but never able to enjoy it.

I remember my kingdom, full of suffering and pain.My people cried out for help, but I turned away.

I was blinded by my greed, my heart was made of stone.But now, I'm the one who's suffering, trapped in this tree alone.

"My branches now bear the weight of my past mistakes

and now because of you I wake up by the blood drop fallen on me tell me who are you what are you doing hear

I'm Joseph. I live in a small village I was a woodcutter, spending long hours in the forest to gather wood that I sell at the market.

Alright, Joseph, I sense that you are a good man, and I will not trouble you further. Take this gold as a gift

"Leave now, and I am bound to this forest, but you are free to live your life.

Go go away from hear and never come again.

Then the Joseph took the gold piece and went to his house and shared the happened story to the Leena she surprised and said is this really happened Joseph said yes Leena its happened and this is the gold piece I bought from the tree, Leena said then sell it we may get some money from it where it is a small piece of gold also Joseph decided to sell the gold . Then Joseph went to sell the gold near goldsmith. The goldsmith tested the gold and surprised it was very pure gold where did you get this gold piece Joseph said I found this piece near river were Joseph lied to the smith because not to tell the story of the golden tree. Joseph received a small amount of money from the goldsmith with that money he purchased food and clothings for his family members

Were Joseph wife and children felt very happy for getting new cloths for them

There happens made Joseph to be more happier than there family members and the day passed and the next day Joseph went for wood cutting and he started his daily routine work while cutting tree he remembered about BHASI BA.

Joseph was started thinking about the tree why can'n I go again and give some blood to tree and bring some gold were I can spend money from the gold that I get from tree. He started his way to reach the tree where he went on the last day. Joseph started walking to reach the tree.after some time Joseph reached the place and standees in front of the tree and think about the words said by the tree "I will give you gold if I get human blood".

Joseph started thinking now how can I get human blood from where I should bring and suddenly he gets a idea why should I hurt my hand with my axe so I can get more blood then i can receive more gold. Joseph took his axe and slightly hurted him self and pour the blood drops on the tree and the tree wakeup making the same kind so sound as it done before the tree BHASE BA wakeup's and the gold was fallen from the tree and Joseph took the gold the BHASE BA started talking Joseph you came again Joseph replayed yes, BHASI BA I came again I need some gold so, i can get some money and I can make my family happy with that money.

BHASI BA replayed to Joseph ok but don't become hunger for money it will kill you but Joseph does not listed to his words he only looking for the gold that fallen from tree .

BHASI BA reply but Joseph don't come again it will cost your blood every time your blood is also important to you not money does not bring every think Joseph said ok I will not come again said to him and took the gold peaces which was fallen from the tree and went to his house and did the same think the he done before and purchase a new house with the money he got from gold and his family felt very happy with the new house.

Joseph started his daily routine work after completing of all the money that he get from gold. He did not think about the tree again were he can get gold. He just living his normal life as he lives before after few days he was not satisfying with the money that he gets from wood selling.i was doing this much hard work but getting very small amount of money why can't I go to BHASI BA again and bring gold again but I already hurted my self what should i do now were I can get blood, Joseph thinking deeply what should I do now then he get a dark idea why my blood should be given why can't I get someones blood to get gold from tree Yes, it was a great idea but if he know he will also ask the share in gold. then he thought why cant i kill any one and I can get more amount of blood and get lot of gold than I can become rich and I can leave happy and no need to work and I can purchase what ever I want and my family needs that can also fulfilled my dreams to yes, this is the right idea to become rich. Joseph did not even realised that he was doing a crime for money he only thinks about the gold, money and to become rich in life.

BLOOD FOR GOLD

Joseph's obsession with the rich life .He started planning to kill his neighbour, an old man to get his blood.

Joseph thought, "If I give more blood to the tree then, it will give me more gold." So, that I can become more rich

One night, Joseph snuck into neighbours house with a knife. He found the old man sleeping and Joseph killed him quietly.

Joseph collected his blood and ran to the forest. He poured the blood on Tree and BHASI BA wakeup's and laughed very loudly I know you will come again for gold this is the thirsty of to being rich no one can change you now you will never get back from this trap but Joseph did not listen to him what he was saying Joseph took the gold and went to house

But his wife, asked you did not get hurt your self how did you get this much of gold where did you get that much of blood

Joseph lied, "I found a body in the forest."

His wife doubted him, but Joseph convinced her to keep quiet.

Now Joseph became one of the richest person from his village and the village people still getting confused were the Joseph is getting this much of money.

Joseph were thinking again and again why can't I get more gold and become even more richer and he planned for another murder.

Joseph wanted more gold, so he planned to kill again. Then He saw a little boy playing alone. Joseph tricked him and took him to the forest

Joseph killed the boy and took his blood. He gave the blood to the tree, BHASI BA The tree gave more gold.

And Joseph continues to kill people for blood....

One day, while Joseph was giving blood to BHASI BA, a villager named Ramesh saw him. Ramesh was out collecting firewood and stumbled upon Joseph pouring blood into the tree's roots.

Ramesh was shocked and hide behind a bush, watching Joseph. He saw the gold appear and Joseph take it.

Ramesh thought, "Joseph is the one who killing our people! He's giving their blood to the tree!" And getting gold

Ramesh ran back to the village and told everyone what he saw. The villagers were angry and scared.

Ramesh went to Joseph's house and found a room filled with gold . The Joseph suddenly came and saw Ramesh

Ramesh got into fight with Joseph,. Unfortunately, Joseph killed Ramesh.

With Ramesh's lifeless body before him, Joseph's greed took over. He took Ramesh's blood and went to Tree BHASE BA

As he poured Ramesh's blood into the tree's roots, He thought, "More gold will be mine!

BHASI BA had a loud laughter, were its branches shaking with a joy. "Foolish Joseph, I warned you not to come again, but you didn't listen! I told you you know what my curse would be broken if someone came more than twice a day , and now you've sealed your fate.

now you'll suffer the same fate as me. You'll be trapped, just like I was, and your become as tree now

"Goodbye, Joseph. Your karma has caught up with you.

BHASI BA finished speaking, its branches wrapped around Joseph, holding him in place. The tree's trunk began to glow, and Joseph felt his soul being pulled into the tree. He realised too late that he had made a terrible mistake.

JOSEPH BECAME LIKE BHASI BA

The villagers, finally free from Joseph's terror, took action. They banished Joseph's family from the village, forcing them to leave behind their homes and belongings.

The villagers were destroyed all of Joseph's properties, including his house and the secret room where he kept his gold. They burned his wealth and all his property.

The village elder declared, "Let this be a lesson to all. Greed and evil will not be tolerated in our village.

As the villagers warning their children of the dangers of greed and the importance of living with kindness.

Written by
SHEKHAR NAYAK

TO YOU THE READER

To you the reader from the deepest part of my heart thank you thank you for picking up this book for choosing to spend your precious time whitin these pages Thank you for being a part of this journey your presence as a reader are the ultimate reward. This book tells what happens in life if you can't over come from fear this book is recommended for children and adults This is the story about the young boy who struggles with fear. His fears hold him back and he finds it hard to overcome them. He's scared of many things, As we follow his journey we see how his fear affects his relationships with his friends and family, his school life, and his daily struggles. This book is now available on Amazon, Flipkart, and NotionPress in various formats, including Paperback, Hardcover, and eBook.

@IAMSHEKHARNAYAK

On instagram as @iamshekharnayak